Lerner SPORTS

I0883005

SPORTS ALL-STARS

JAYSON TATUM

Jon M. Fishman

Lerner Publications ◆ Minneapolis

Lerner Publications Company
An imprint of Lerner Publishing Group, Inc.
241 First Avenue North
Minneapolis, MN 55401 USA

For reading levels and more information, look up this title at www.lernerbooks.com.

Main body text set in Albany Std. Typeface provided by Agfa.

Editor: Brianna Kaiser **Photo Editor:** Brianna Kaiser

Library of Congress Cataloging-in-Publication Data

Names: Fishman, Jon M., author.
Title: Jayson Tatum / Jon M. Fishman.
Description: Minneapolis : Lerner Publications, [2022] | Series: Sports all-stars (Lerner sports) | Includes bibliographical references and index. | Audience: Ages 7–11 | Audience: Grades 2–3 | Summary: "Meet Jayson Tatum, power forward and small forward for the Boston Celtics. From his training schedule to what he does off the court, readers will learn all about this NBA All-Star"—Provided by publisher.
Identifiers: LCCN 2021000110 (print) | LCCN 2021000111 (ebook) | ISBN 9781728404394 (hardcover) | ISBN 9781728423104 (paperback) | ISBN 9781728418858 (ebook)
Subjects: LCSH: Tatum, Jayson, 1998– —Juvenile literature. | Basketball players—United States—Biography—Juvenile literature.
Classification: LCC GV884.T375 2022 (print) | LCC GV884.T375 2022 (ebook) | DDC 796.323092 [B]—dc23

LC record available at https://lccn.loc.gov/2021000110
LC ebook record available at https://lccn.loc.gov/2021000111

Manufactured in the United States of America
1-48497-49011-4/12/2021

TABLE OF CONTENTS

A FIGHTING CHANCE

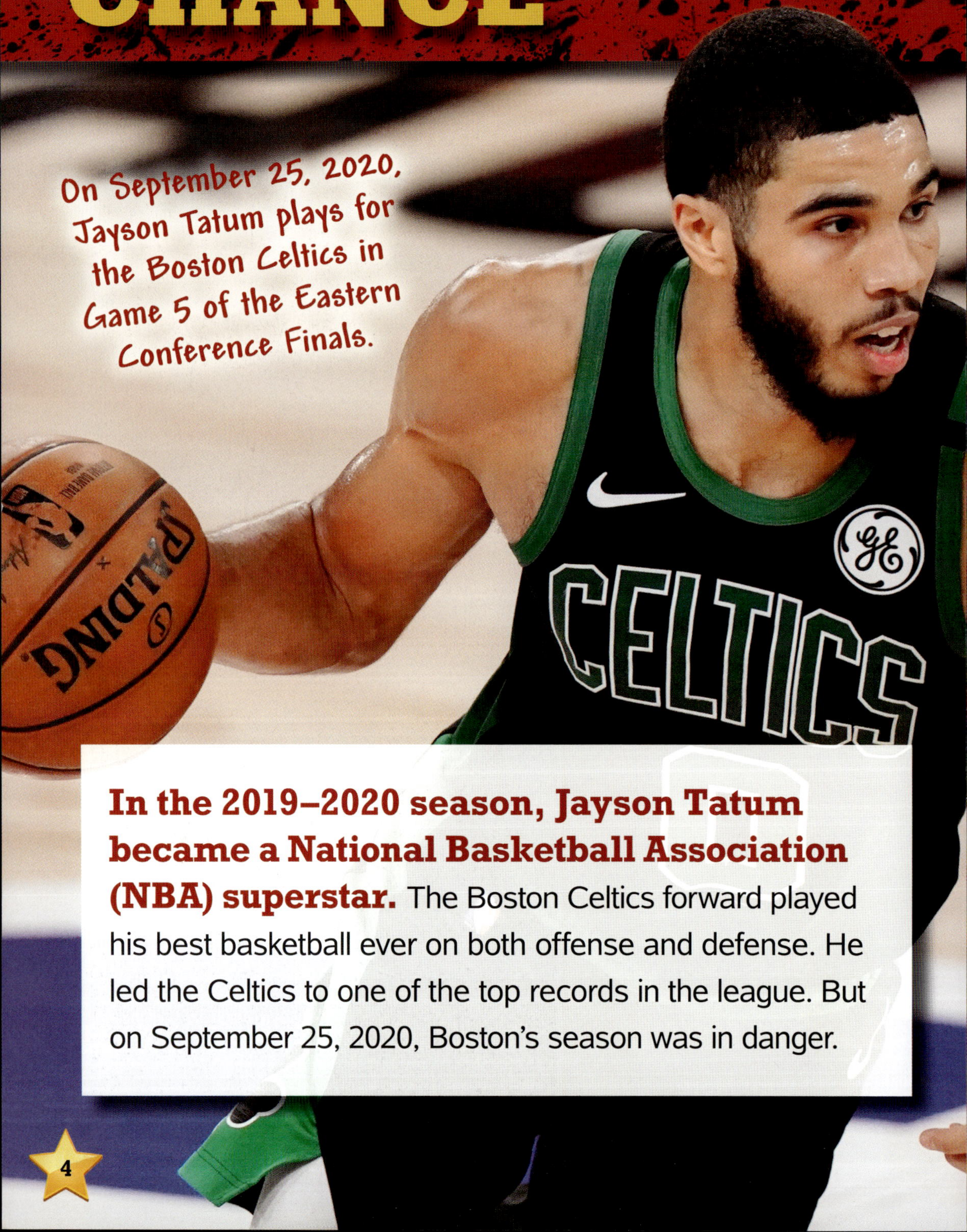

On September 25, 2020, Jayson Tatum plays for the Boston Celtics in Game 5 of the Eastern Conference Finals.

In the 2019–2020 season, Jayson Tatum became a National Basketball Association (NBA) superstar. The Boston Celtics forward played his best basketball ever on both offense and defense. He led the Celtics to one of the top records in the league. But on September 25, 2020, Boston's season was in danger.

FACTS AT A GLANCE

- **Date of birth:** March 3, 1998
- **Position:** forward
- **League:** NBA
- **Professional highlights:** selected by the Boston Celtics with the third overall pick in the 2017 NBA Draft; led the Celtics to the Eastern Conference Finals in 2018 and 2020; led the Celtics in scoring in 2020
- **Personal highlights:** practiced being a famous athlete with his mother; played one season at Duke University; became a father in 2017

Tatum shoots and scores against the Miami Heat.

The team trailed the Miami Heat by two games in the Eastern Conference Finals. If the Celtics lost Game 5, their season would be over. Yet with everything on the line, Boston had a rough start. They missed 11 of their first 12 shots. At halftime, Miami had a 58–51 lead.

Tatum knew his team had to fight harder in the second half. "It's not going to be perfect," he said. "You just want to give yourself a chance."

After halftime, Tatum did just that. He grabbed rebounds and made free throws. He sank a long shot from behind the three-point line. The 26-foot (8 m) basket gave Boston an eight-point lead.

Tatum scored 17 points in the third quarter to help put his team ahead by nine points. In the fourth quarter, the Celtics kept scoring and playing tough defense. They won the game 121–108.

Tatum was the game's top scorer with 31 points. He added 10 rebounds and six assists to help the Celtics win. The victory kept Boston's season alive for another day. If Tatum could lead his team to two more wins, the Celtics would reach the NBA Finals.

DECISION MAKER

Tatum drives to the basket for the Duke Blue Devils on December 6, 2016.

Jayson Tatum grew up in St. Louis, Missouri. He lived with his mother, Brandy Cole. His father, Justin Tatum, lived nearby and played basketball for Saint Louis University. He went on to play pro basketball in the Netherlands. Jayson and his father talked on the phone almost every day.

Growing up, Tatum lived with his mother in St. Louis, Missouri.

Cole attended the University of Missouri–St. Louis. Jayson was too young to stay home alone, so Cole often brought him with her to class. “I just did what a lot of moms have to do,” she said. “We just figured it out, made decisions.”

At an early age, Jayson dreamed of being a pro basketball player. He practiced shooting with a small hoop attached to his bathtub with suction cups. He told his mother that when he grew up he wanted to be like Los Angeles Lakers superstar Kobe Bryant.

Jayson loved basketball, and he worked hard to get better. His height also helped him stand out during games. "I remember after first grade, he was always taller than his teachers," his mother said. Being tall helped Jayson shoot over defenders and reach high for rebounds. He was usually one of the tallest players on the court.

In 2012, Jayson attended high school at Chaminade College Preparatory School. He averaged 13.3 points and 6.4 rebounds per game in his first season with the varsity team. He kept growing, and he got better every year. In 2015–2016, his senior season at Chaminade, he averaged 29.6 points and 9.1 rebounds per game.

Standing at 6 feet 8 (2 m), Tatum is still one of the tallest players on the court. The average height for an NBA player is about 6 feet 6 (2 m).

Tatum plays for Chaminade's basketball team on January 18, 2016.

Jayson's size and skill impressed everyone who saw him play. College scouts liked how much he had improved during high school. Many colleges around the United States, from Arizona to Connecticut, wanted Jayson to play for their teams. He decided to attend Duke University in Durham, North Carolina.

In 2016–2017, Tatum played 29 games with the Duke Blue Devils. He averaged 16.8 points and 7.3 rebounds per game. Both stats ranked second on the team.

After one season at Duke, Tatum was ready for the next level. He entered the 2017 NBA Draft and was one step closer to achieving his lifelong dream. On June 22, the Celtics chose him with the third overall pick. By reaching the NBA, he'd completed his dream. After the draft, he set out to become a league superstar.

Tatum poses with his Celtics jersey after the NBA Draft in 2017.

PRACTICE MAKES PERFECT

Tatum practices shooting before a game in high school.

To give himself the best chance to reach the NBA, Tatum began training when he was a kid. The NBA has 30 teams that each have 15 players. Since only 450 people can play in the league at a time, the competition for open roster slots is fierce.

Working on shooting helps Tatum prepare for success in games.

Tatum was talented, but having natural talent isn't always enough. He would have to work really hard to make it.

Tatum spent time with his father's teams. He watched how the players got ready for games. He listened to what the coaches said and learned what it took to be a top player.

Tall basketball players often focus on grabbing rebounds and scoring near the basket. But with his father's help, Tatum worked on dribbling and shooting

Tatum dribbles during a game in 2018.

from long distance. Both skills are huge parts of his success and set him apart from many other tall players.

In high school, Tatum's mornings were almost always the same. He awoke at 5 a.m. and left home at 5:30. At the Chaminade gym, he worked out for 90 minutes and took 250 shots before school started. His coach, Frank Bennett, said Tatum hardly ever missed a day of morning practice.

Tatum trained even harder in college. Before beginning his freshman year at Duke, he started working out with his new teammates. They lifted weights and practiced yoga together. And they played a lot of basketball, often practicing late into the night.

At Duke, Tatum ate healthful foods prepared by a team chef. But tacos are his favorite thing to eat. That's why one of his nicknames is Taco Jay.

After joining the NBA, Tatum got some training help from one of his heroes. In 2018, he received a message from Kobe Bryant. Bryant said he was happy for Tatum's success and offered to work out with him. The next summer, Tatum met Bryant for a workout. Bryant showed Tatum some moves and gave him tips to improve. "I'll never forget that day, how I felt going into the workout, how I felt afterward," Tatum said. "I just felt like that was the coolest thing ever for me."

Kobe Bryant plays for the Los Angeles Lakers in 2003.

READY FOR ANYTHING

Tatum shoots in a game against the Philadelphia 76ers on August 23, 2020.

Like most NBA stars, Tatum spends a lot of time talking to the media. Players do interviews for TV shows and magazine stories. Reporters ask questions before and after games. Some players feel uneasy with all the attention. But thanks to his mother, Tatum was ready for it.

Tatum practiced answering interviews with his mother (*left*) when he was young.

Growing up, Tatum learned to expect surprise interviews. While holding a hairbrush like a microphone, his mother would fire questions at him to answer. Cole said she wanted her son to be prepared for the NBA's spotlight. As one of the world's top players, he's ready to answer any question thrown his way.

In November 2020, Tatum put his media skills to use. The Celtics agreed to a new contract with their star player. The five-year deal was worth $195 million. Tatum told reporters that he loved Boston and was thrilled to play there for five more years.

Tatum answers interview questions in 2017.

Tatum grabs a rebound in 2020.

Deuce

On December 6, 2017, Tatum and Toriah Lachell welcomed their son, Jayson Christopher Tatum Jr., to the world. Most people call him Deuce. He isn't an official member of the Celtics, but he's an important part of the team.

Deuce often hangs out in the locker room and talks to the players. After games, he goes onto the court and answers questions with his dad. Even when Deuce isn't at the arena, Tatum thinks about him often. The name Deuce is written on the tongues of the shoes Tatum wears during games.

Tatum holds his son, Deuce, after a game in 2020.

Tatum uses some of his money to help his community. The Jayson Tatum Foundation puts on basketball camps for kids. The camps teach kids to work hard, set goals, and help one another. Campers also get to play plenty of basketball.

In 2018, Tatum answers kids' questions at the Jayson Tatum Basketball ProCamp.

The Jayson Tatum Foundation started the Daddy & Deuce Toy & Coat Drive in 2018. At the drives, workers gather winter clothes for people who need them. Workers also collect school supplies, books, and toys to give to children and families.

"ANYTHING IS POSSIBLE"

Tatum (*left*) keeps his eyes on the basket as he dribbles the ball.

During his first NBA season in 2017–2018, Tatum averaged 13.9 points, five rebounds, and 1.6 assists per game. In his second season, he improved each of those stats. He totaled 15.7 points, six rebounds, and 2.1 assists per game. Similar to his improvement in high school, Tatum was getting better each year in the NBA.

Tatum shoots over Marc Gasol of the Toronto Raptors on September 4, 2020.

In 2020, a new disease, COVID-19, spread around the world. To help slow the spread, the NBA stopped playing in March. Players suddenly had a lot of free time on their hands.

During the time off, Tatum kept practicing and working out. When games resumed in July, he felt stronger than

Tatum shoots in Game 4 of the 2020 Eastern Conference Finals.

ever. He was ready to play like a true NBA superstar. "I can get better at everything," he said.

Tatum did get better at everything. He averaged 23.4 points, seven rebounds, and three assists per game. The Celtics had a 48–24 record, third best in the Eastern Conference. But in the Eastern Conference Finals, Boston fell to the Heat in six games.

The Celtics are tied with the Los Angeles Lakers for the most NBA championships (17). The Lakers won the title in 2020, but the Celtics haven't won it since 2008.

Tatum is ready to lead the Celtics to their next NBA title. As a kid, he had big dreams, and he has achieved most of them as an adult. He wants others to know they can too. "If you have a dream, always hold onto that . . . no matter where you're from, how your life started growing up," he said. "Anything is possible."

Tatum dunks in 2020.

All-Star Stats

Some NBA players are great shooters or passers but don't play strong defense. Others grab a lot of rebounds but don't score many points. Tatum does it all. Look at how he compared to his 2019–2020 teammates in three key stats.

Points scored per game

1.	Jayson Tatum	23.4
2.	Kemba Walker	20.4
3.	Jaylen Brown	20.3
4.	Gordon Hayward	17.5
5.	Marcus Smart	12.9

Rebounds per game

1.	Enes Kanter	7.4
2.	Jayson Tatum	7.0
3.	Gordon Hayward	6.7
4.	Daniel Theis	6.6
5.	Jaylen Brown	6.4

Assists per game

1.	Marcus Smart	4.9
2.	Kemba Walker	4.8
3.	Gordon Hayward	4.1
4.	Jayson Tatum	3.0
5.	Brad Wanamaker	2.5

Glossary

assist: a pass that leads directly to a score

conference: a group of teams

draft: when teams take turns choosing new players

forward: a player who usually plays near the basket

free throw: an unguarded shot from behind the foul line awarded by the referee after a foul

rebound: catching a basketball after a missed shot

roster: a list of players on a team

scout: a person who judges the skills of athletes

varsity: the top team at a school

yoga: exercises that promote mind and body health

Source Notes

6 Associated Press, "Celtics Control Second Half, Top Heat to Win Game 5 in East," *ESPN*, September 25, 2020, https://www.espn.com/nba/recap?gameId=401247146.

9 "Rising Celtics Star Jayson Tatum Continues to Find Inspiration from His Mother," CBS Boston, May 23, 2018, https://boston.cbslocal.com/2018/05/23/jayson-tatum-mother-brandy-cole-boston-celtics-nba/.

10 Jonathan Adams, "Jayson Tatum's Family: 5 Fast Facts You Need to Know," Heavy, May 9, 2018, https://heavy.com/sports/2017/06/jayson-tatum-family-parents-dad-mom-siblings-stats-height-bio/.

17 Justin Leger, "Celtics' Jayson Tatum Reflects on 'Surreal' Workout with Kobe Bryant," Yahoo Entertainment, August 13, 2020, https://www.yahoo.com/entertainment/celtics-jayson-tatum-reflects-surreal-015544111.html.

26 John Karalis, "Boston Celtics Jayson Tatum Adds Muscle, Take Game 'Up Another Level,' 'I Can Get Better at Everything,'" MassLive, July 11, 2020, https://www.masslive.com/celtics/2020/07/boston-celtics-jayson-tatum-adds-muscle-take-game-up-another-level-i-can-get-better-at-everything.html.

27 Mike Simone, "Gatorade Athlete of the Year Award Winner Jayson Tatum on Focus, Fitness, and Living Your Dream," *Men's Journal*, accessed December 19, 2020, https://www.mensjournal.com/sports/gatorade-athlete-year-award-winner-jayson-tatum-focus-fitness-and-living-your/.

Learn More

Clausen-Grace, Nicki, and Jeff Grace. *Boston Celtics*. Mankato, MN: Black Rabbit Books, 2021.

The Jayson Tatum Foundation
https://thejaysontatumfoundation.org

Jayson Tatum—NBA.com
https://www.nba.com/player/1628369/jayson_tatum

Leed, Percy. *Kobe Bryant: NBA Champion*. Minneapolis: Lerner Publications, 2021.

Monson, James. *Behind the Scenes Basketball*. Minneapolis: Lerner Publications, 2020.

Sports Illustrated Kids—Basketball
https://www.sikids.com/basketball

Index

Photo Acknowledgments

Image credits: AP Photo/Mark J. Terrill, pp. 4–5, 6, 21, 25, 26; AP Photo/Rich Graessle, p. 8; Daniel Schwen/Wikimedia Commons (CC 4.0), p. 9; AP Photo/Gregory Payan, pp. 11, 13; AP Photo/Charles Krupa, p. 12; AP Photo/Rick Bowmer, p. 14; AP Photo/Gerry Broome, p. 15; AP Photo/Kevork Djansezian, p. 17; AP Photo/Kim Klement, p. 18; Barry King/Alamy Stock Photo, p. 19; AP Photo/Frank Franklin II, p. 20; AP Photo/Elise Amendola, p. 22; AP Photo/Cristina M. Fletes, p. 23; AP Photo/Lynne Sladky, p. 24; AP Photo/Michael Dwyer, p. 27.

Cover: AP Photo/Charles Krupa.